TO THE

GREAT
SEA

A Story for Christmas

DOUG THOMPSON

Matador
9 Priory Business Park
Kibworth Beauchamp
Leicestershire LE8 0RX, UK
Tel: (+44) 116 279 2299
Fax: (+44) 116 279 2277
Email: books@troubador.co.uk
Web: www.troubador.co.uk/matador

ISBN 978 1848767 706

British Library Cataloguing in Publication Data.
A catalogue record for this book is available from the British Library.

Typeset in 12pt Aldine401 Roman by Troubador Publishing Ltd, Leicester, UK
Printed and bound in the UK by TJ International, Padstow, Cornwall

Matador is an imprint of Troubador Publishing Ltd

TO THE GREAT SEA

All in an instant, we become aware that a deep change has overtaken us and our fortunes. It is a change whose gathering has been anything but sudden; slow, persistent, well-nigh imperceptible, cocooned within the comfort of all that is familiar, like a cancer in the body.

And now, in the garden, in the heat of the day, a harsh new light freezes the mottling shadows and dusk ushers in a malevolent breeze, whispering fear among leaves and branches.

Yet no word comes, no shattering voice; only sudden, desperate, momentary listening; backward glances; the pall of silence.

And when at last we can bear this fearful waiting no

longer, we flee its palpable menace beyond our known horizons, into the dark lands.

It is a bitter parting.

Abandoning the southward road almost at once, we turn west and reach the broad river some little time before dawn. At the crossing, a boatman huddled in a blanket at the stern. Shaking him gently my servant rouses him, so gently, I think he carries us over with the dream still lingering in his heavy eyes. And in truth, once out of the reeds onto the bobbing river, amid swirling drifts of mist, which accompany us over the water, the hollow creak and boom of the paddle's quiet rhythm seems to echo us too into the antechamber of a ferryman's dream.

At the first village, a little way beyond the river, we try to buy animals, sufficient for our journey across the wide stony waste, and to hire drovers returning to Damascus or the more distant coast.

Waiting in the thin, early-morning sunlight among trees, at the end of the village, I see my man, Rastim, returning empty handed. There are none to be had. The village is too poor, he says. But I mark his still puckered brow, and wonder why it is he has not told me all. Skirting the last houses, we turn south again, hoping to meet with better fortune along the great caravan route going down into Arabia from the northern lands.

Many hours of hard riding bring us within sight of a small town, and just before reaching its gates we fall in with a long line of merchants, as though we are of their company. The bustling crowds bear us along the noisy street, spilling us out into the market place where at once we are gladdened by the sight of animals in plenty, and here and there among the throng, also of black-cloaked drovers from the lands by the Great Sea's edge.

Hunger and thirst, however, compel us first, and there, in the tavern, as we pick over the poor fare, we hear, without ever quite listening, the drifting words of those who pass near us or those who sit or stand in groups round about us. Snatches of traders' talk: the rise and fall of prices, the shortages of homespun, of wine or spices; the whispered wars, the fortune or fall of satraps and princes – only half attended as we beckon for more wine and break our bread.

Through the comings and goings, I glimpse a knot of drovers, and motioning to Rastim not to rise, push forward myself to where they crouch, dicing by the open door. None of them is engaged, they confess, nor is like to be, until the brightly burning star that nightly flames across the troubled sky is done with havoc and passes on into the endless blackness whence it came. None would move. Daily their provisions dwindle, ruined whether they leave or stay, yet they would not move.

"How long?" I ask, "before this star you so much dread drops into the void that lies beyond the horizon of its homing?"

"One whole moon at least," says one.

"More likely two or three; who knows these things for sure?" opines his neighbour.

"This star," I say, curious to know, "what evils has it

wrought that you have seen?"

Each looks to the other, yet no one speaks. Their silence grows like an ache between us. I pity, whilst also despising, their down-turned eyes and shuffling feet, and I press them sorely – "You have seen nothing, then?"

At last, someone speaks up, telling of a cock new-slaughtered crowing twice; then another of a lamb born with two heads and each did devour the other; yet another of a camel drinking long and deep, yet on the first day's journey dead of thirst; and so of the earth which shook, and the noonday sun that withered in an instant into night; of the coming of a king who would sweep away the Powers of the Earth... I turn away and leave them to their portents and their dice.

And through the doorway, I observe the wintry sun, opaque and wan, withdrawn into an ivory sky, minutely grained with porphyry, a baleful eye whose cold white stare bears in upon me the certainty that this is all folly; the worst time of year for a journey.

Cast into this unwonted freedom by a nameless fear, I

am become as a felucca without sail or tiller, compelled by winds and waters; I who have lived always to shape, to order and direct, awful instrument of the One Great Design, myself an aimless wanderer now.

It was then my servant confessed that in the village, in the morning, he had heard the same story. All had cowered at the slow, nightly passage of this harbinger of sorrows, petrifier of all that lay in the wake of its crystal fire. Nevertheless, in spite of this, we must be gone, for the silent wrath which stalks us may even now be at the gates.

The faithful Rastim, nodding gravely, stood at once and stepped away into the ailing light of that winter's afternoon. How long he is away I cannot say, but by the time he returns darkness has all but devoured the day and made us its captive. Two men of Tarsus, brothers, would accompany us, he says, "but they are demanding more than the customary wages…"

My protest is at once silenced, reminded by Rastim that they are the only two he can find who are willing to leave.

We would depart at first light and thus must contract now for animals, skins for water, and all our provender, as well as beds for the night. How curious – I quickly learn – the miraculous effect this bringer of catastrophes has on prices! Wry looks, shrugging shoulders, wringing hands and heavenward glances are all in season now, regrets are legion, as are excuses. Logic of the maggot, I aver, while proffering yet more silver.

Late in the night I leave my blankets and climb the outer stairs to the roof. The murky gloom of morning and afternoon has yielded to peerless clarity. The mantle of Mithra is spread out in all its majesty, awesome and endless. The air is crisp as water from the fissured well of Anahita, and already the snow is faintly falling, feathery on the pathless uplands, which must bring us to the Great Western Sea.

A cold coming we would have of it, for sure. I crouch beneath the parapet and draw my cloak tightly about me. Frost glints through the darkness, caught by starlight. I hunt the heavens, finding this new, fateful

7

messenger of Mithra almost at once, already a little way beyond, veering away west and south, brighter and nearer than all the rest. Contemplating its slow, dreamlike, brightly glistening passage across the star-flowered plain of the firmament, I marvel yet again at the habitual, gaping blackness in the worm-filled souls that fill the vacant spaces all about us. And yet – and I smile at the thought – here am I now, between somewhere and nowhere, sometime and never, scurrying away, hiding from shadows!

And yet again, this star, which is itself fire, cleaves its furrow between darkness and darkness, dividing earth into shadows and yet more shadows, with the passing of its light.

Then suddenly, a goat bleating in the first wisps of dawn breaks in upon my musings, and anxious voices below, scurrying feet, lamps being fetched and lit, doors opening and banging shut within. Cries in a language I do not comprehend.

What propositions, I wonder, does all this chancing together make in a cold, dreary dawn?

I stand up stiffly, stretch, and peer out over the parapet into the courtyard below. Three men in a huddle, together in the half light, while a boy darts briskly from door to door. Then a cry of recognition. One of the figures, breaking away towards me, and pointing, "He is found. On the roof. Look!" Only then does it come to me that my empty blankets were the cause of this sudden turmoil.

I descend in a trice and the three men hurry towards me. Vexed, as much by my own thoughtlessness as at his solicitude, I push Rastim aside. "Pay the reckoning and let us be gone; the sun will soon be up."

While he is yet indoors, I step out into the street beyond the arch, deserted except for our tethered beasts and the small flock of sheep and goats pressed up against the inn wall under the watchful eye of a huge dog, a lion almost. The two Tarsians follow me and stand at a respectful distance as I choose the camel I shall ride and busy myself tightening its harness.

When my servant at last comes out into the street

he speaks first and briefly with the drovers. Then he approaches me, smiling. "All is paid, Lord, and all is ready."

I signal my approval. "Then let us be gone."

"To Damascus is it, Lord?" he inquires.

His question, foolishly, takes me unawares, and I stand a while, pondering it. At length, I shake my head. "My... purposes... are changed. I first have business far to the south. We make for Jerusalem."

Rastim is visibly startled.

"Inform the Tarsians," I bid him, "... and say I shall pay them well."

In the fast gathering light I observe their faces and their gestures and see their anger rising. Then one of them, the elder – it transpires – pushes past my servant, strides towards me and stands squarely before me.

"We contracted for Damascus, sir. What sudden change is this? Mah has risen, shed her light and faded many times since last we saw our homeland. Too many times! We now wish to return there with all speed. Damascus is in our path. Jerusalem is a very different matter." And after a slight pause, "Besides, sir… this star men fear, it too is moving towards Jerusalem…"

Anger grips my throat sharply. I regard him steadily, looking into his eyes, before answering, yet he does not flinch away, I notice. "*I* do not fear this star. However, as it is men I need, not anxious, worried women, take whatever payment is your due and go your way. I shall find others who have more courage…"

He is smiling, almost imperceptibly smiling. I see him even now. His voice is calm and steady. I hear it, even now. "My brother and I have been away much too long, sir. This wandering life is for young men and we are no longer young. We want no more of it." Again he pauses, perhaps inviting my comment. But I remain silent. "The star I mention for your sake, sir, not ours. All men fear something at some time… even great lords and kings. Just now many fear this star. For us it is merely… a star… seeking its peace."

I realise, in this moment, I have sorely misjudged him, have presumed a mere drover, not a man. Nor was there any trace of *arak* on his breath… I knew then

11

I must try another way. "And when you have done with all this, what then?" I ask him.

"We know about goats and sheep, which we shall rear, and live out the remainder of our lives with our wives and growing sons… having found our peace."

I can only nod in this moment, struck by his quiet confidence, his forthrightness; then recovering, I probe further, "You have land and herds already?"

At this he shook his head. "No, we have neither; yet we have not squandered… We shall manage well enough, I think."

I considered him awhile, weighing my thoughts carefully before shaping them into words. "If you and your brother were to come with us to Jerusalem I promise I would release you there, making no further demands, and pay you the price of… of… twenty ewes… a pair of rams and… twenty goats… if such be indeed the substance of your dream of peace."

Every man, I believed then, has his price, and I waited with cynical curiosity to see whether I had pitched his aright.

A certain look, even before he answered, told me plainly that I had not yet gained the measure of the man.

"For a man like you sir, I suspect... such numbers are... as nothing, plucked out of the air... from nowhere. That a man's 'dream of peace' can have mere dumb beasts at its centre is, I think, beyond your comprehension... contemptible perhaps. For my brother and me – as you well surmise – such numbers represent almost half a lifetime's labour. Half a lifetime! Just think of that, sir. Half a lifetime of wandering through these wastelands, back and forth, living in tents; the heat and the cold, the dust, the sores, the sandstorms, the flies, and worst of all, always... another's behest... A man like you cannot possibly have any conception of what that means, because it is totally outside your experience. Perhaps at the end of this journey, if indeed you do undertake this journey, you will begin to know something of what it means. And yet, and forgive me for saying so... even then, nothing depends on it for you; you can give it up at will, go back to your... summer palace, to your silken girls bringing sherbet, and amuse yourself with some different... whim, something not quite so uncomfortable... nor so dangerous. But for us, sir, this is our life. This is life..."

He stood his ground, looking me straight in the eye, quite unperturbed. And seeing that I made no response, he went on: "Your numbers abound with this world's injustices, sir, not least because you would be *giving* nothing, knowing full well that for us it was... all."

His words sting like the scorpion's tail and with that same sharp sense of truth, yet – even though I know it diminishes me – I cannot withhold a sneering "but you will accept, nay, *grasp* at them all the same, will you not, for all your philosophising, unjust or no!"

He stepped back then, two or three paces, and again regarded me steadily before speaking. "I shall tell my brother what you purpose... but I do not doubt we shall accept. How can we not accept? The heavens would never open twice to pour forth their bounty on such as us… But… permit me one last question, sir… Would such a 'miracle' as this be even thinkable for you, sir?"

I did not immediately appreciate the meaning behind the question and he must have read the perplexity in my look.

"I see I do not make myself clear. What I mean is this… plainly speaking: What would be the substance of your 'dream of peace'? For with you too, most surely, it is only a dream… For why else would you be making this hazardous journey?"

To my great relief, with a peremptory bow, he turned away then, without insisting on an answer.

This land we enter now mocks the hand of Mithra. It is truly the Anti-Ghaion, where earth and air, fire and water all wither finally into ash, forever dwindling and dissolving between the summer sun's noonday rage and wintry moon-tide's icy fire, winnowed by a nithering wind that flays the last strips of flesh from the earth's carcass.

Endless echoing miles over rock and sand. A world of substance made insubstantial. Crags and peaks like broken, yellow teeth, stark against a leering void. Wind moaning or howling, a ravening jackal tearing at these hollow ribs. Scree stones skittering away in a moment only to settle into new, millennial silences. Grey opacity; cloud-smoke scudding, now whirling, now eddying; momentarily glimpsing the sun's sickly mien. Silent peaks, jagged pinnacles of rock, lurching towards us like shattered souls at the last extremity. Broken lines, faded hues, voiding mists; like the final forgetting. And in the upland coombs an icy gloom, drifts of snow, a sallow, impalpable world. The ways deep, the cold sharp, the days short; the very dead of winter.

On the third day we became aware that we were not the only travellers over that dreary landscape; and at once the gnawing fear rushed back within me.

We are moving along the southern side of a wide *wadi*, which we had crossed late on the previous afternoon, when my servant falls back to warn me that the Tarsians think they have heard the jingling of harnesses on the further side, but the mist is heavy, the distance too great to be sure. Much later, when fear of pursuit is once again withdrawing into the further crannies of my mind, the elder Tarsian comes to me. "A little way ahead, the *wadi* narrows – though by good fortune, it also deepens – and at that point, through the gloom, I glimpsed the shapes of men and camels, many men and many camels; but the dark air, the swirling snowflakes swallowed them in an instant. Yet they are there. For certain, they are there."

I nodded, and thanked him. "How far ahead?" I asked.

"Perhaps five, six hundred paces, no more." And he eased away towards his brother who was just then coming up out of the mist with our small herd that was firmly held in check by the great dog, circling them closely, darting or feinting at stragglers.

When he came back my decision was already made. "Let us turn south, away from the *wadi*. At nightfall we shall rest a few hours, moving on again when Mah is at the zenith and the air is clearer. We shall thereafter journey by night and rest in the daytime. That way we shall soon lose them, I think."

But it was not to be. Although we changed direction, travelling mostly at night, always we sensed their nearness, a threatening shadow. Then a little before dawn – it must have been on the sixth day – nearing the top of a sheer-sided defile we saw, too late, their still shadowy forms, stretched out in a line across the opening at the top.

They were waiting for us.

As we gained the lip of the slope these riders closed silently about us and brought us presently to a great black tent, which stood close in beneath the towering wall of rock. I saw by their dress they were from one of the northern satrapies, and was much perplexed by this. The snow, I remember, lay in frozen islands all about us, but it was impossible to see more than fifty paces in any direction, so heavy was the shroud of mist. As we neared the tent they motioned us to dismount and one of them, who had ridden on ahead, now came forward, beckoning us to enter.

On the threshold, I remember thinking that this was surely more than just a captain of the palace guard and in that momentary realisation my gnawing fear was changed in an instant into hope, bewilderment into curiosity. At the last moment I signalled to the others not to follow. Inside, my surmise was at once confirmed. The rock floor was strewn with sumptuous rugs and at the far side there was a pile of silken cushions before which stood a small, wrinkled man. He was smiling quizzically.

I give the customary greeting and he, with a slight movement of his hand, commands the bowl of scented water and the towel, traditional tokens of hospitality among the peoples of the northern lands. This ritual over, he invites me to take my place on the cushions opposite where he himself – I surmise – resumes his place.

"We had a notion you were following us," he began. Then after a pause, "until we saw that you were only four and could therefore pose no threat to us." My relief at his words must have been obvious, for he raised an eyebrow, searching my face, requiring an explanation, which I gave him.

When I had finished he shook his head, observing, "What a sad indictment of our common humanity that even in the maw of desolation we can only approach one another in fear and mistrust." He reflected for a moment on his words, still shaking his head slowly from side to side. Then he looked up. "But we realised, after watching you closely for two nights and two days, that what you are following is not us at all, but what we too follow – the bright voyaging star, I mean."

I smiled and nodded, much relieved. "In a manner of speaking, yes, we are…"

Again he looks puzzled, and it is now that I become suddenly aware of how, without coercion or interrogation, this wily old stranger might find a way to the innermost chambers of a man's soul. Warily now, I tell him the story of my journey thus far, full in detail, yet speaking not at all about my hasty departure from the great city, dwelling rather on the unspecified if urgent business, which leads me to Jerusalem. He follows my words with keen attention, occasionally interrupting to comment or seek clarification, but when I have finished he observes, casually it seems: "It must indeed be a pressing matter that takes you to Jerusalem, away from the once great, though still remarkable city of a thousand gardens... in the very depths of winter."

But I stay silent now, refusing to be drawn further. When he sees that I have indeed concluded my account of our journey, he speaks again. "I was once in your city, you know? – Almost twenty years ago, it would be. I had gone there to look for some ancient scrolls I believed might still be found there... which I desperately wanted to consult." He breaks off abruptly and I look up, my curiosity aroused.

"What scrolls? And did you find them?"

"Not then, no. Though somewhat later I was successful in obtaining copies of several of them... at Persepolis. However, my visit was rewarded in other ways, not least by other, equally interesting manuscripts which came before me there, as I searched. Documents which, in part, explain why I too am to be found, an old man, wandering through these wintry wastes, very far from home…"

Again he paused, and this time I implored him to continue, which he would not do until it had been established that we should now travel on together, and until my servant Rastim and the two Tarsians had been made comfortable, according to their station.

This business done, he went on. "Know then that I am Melichior, a citizen of Ninevah, one time High Priest of Zoroaster in that city, but now… indeed for many years… withdrawn from public life. A seeker after truth."

I gasped, not able to prevent myself exclaiming my wonder – and admiration – for the case of Melichior, the Magus Melichior, was well-known, legendary almost, throughout the Empire.

"I see," he went on, without any trace of pride in his voice or words, "that my name is not unknown to you."

I shook my head, smiling all the while... " But this chance meeting... in the midst of all this desolation... It is incredible! Nothing less than incredible!"

He made no comment, merely nodded, paused a while longer, then went on: "But yes... the scrolls... Many lives of men past, more than ten, perhaps even more than twenty, when your city was at the very height of its power, a power it had wrested from my own city, it was the practice of your triumphant King Nebuchadnezzar to bring captive to his city as many of the powerful families of the lands he had conquered as had been spared the barbarous cruelty of his soldiers. For he reasoned that without their natural leaders a defeated people would long remain submissive to his will. But then, you are surely aware of all of this without my reminding you of it... However, what you may not know is that among these many captives was a certain man of Judea, who rose to be one of the most powerful, trusted and revered of all the king's advisers. It was the writings of this man – his reputed writings – I set out to locate, not – I hasten to add – because his power interested me, rather because of the legends... the mystery... that surrounded him."

In truth, I was only very vaguely aware of the Judean Captivity in our long history, indeed, history itself was of little interest to me, for what was past was past – and poetry, with its unsuspected, stalking truths, was ever then all my study.

"You must understand that by that time, having already achieved the highest power, I was acutely aware of its true worth, and was even then engaged in seeking another way, which was not the way of arrogance, ambition, aggression and triviality – the slippery path I had hitherto trodden so ably and so... wastefully. A lesson" – and here, suddenly, he looked me in the eye – "which you have also begun to learn, if I am not mistaken."

His candour and his perception unnerved me, for what had I said or done in the short time we had been in each other's presence to give these things away? He smiled, a knowing smile, then went on with his story.

"As I have told you, I did not then find his

scriptures. What I did find, however, more than compensated for that disappointment. The captivity of Judea must have been almost total and the integration of its chief families into our own way of life, very considerable. Many of the writings, which they had brought with them into captivity, and which in the course of time I discovered, absorbed my attention and time to such a degree that I must confess I neglected all else for them, completely failing to explore the antiquities and still considerable, legendary beauties of your city.

You see... It was *their* beliefs, attitudes and customs – many of which have long since become our own – which were, ironically, the true victors in Nebuchadnezzar's wars – but then, that happens in so many wars, does it not?"

There was some commotion outside, just then: a jingling of harnesses and prolonged grunting of camels, some cursing, a clashing of metal upon metal. For a moment or two we were distracted, then Melichior explained that the camels were being fed and bedded down until nightfall. It was then, too, that he remembered my people again and called in his chamberlain to make sure that they had indeed been accommodated. When his man had withdrawn, he resumed his seat on the cushions.

"Now, where was I? Ah yes… Among these writings, some of which were historical, some religious or political in character, there were those of a man much given to prophecy – not market-place soothsaying, not that, you understand, but one who claimed the direct inspiration of their god, Yahweh. Being at that time taken up with the problem of purging the arrogance in my own soul, I was quick to detect it in another, and thus I read his words, full of scepticism, scorn even, though the more I read (and he wrote at great length) the more compelling I found his message. Of course, he was a man, and thus not naturally given to humility. He had found Truth, and as the discoverer of Truth, in his pride he secretly felt himself to be as important as his discovery. I say 'secretly' for though he never said it outright, his words nonetheless proclaimed it. Yet, for all that, in the end I had forgiven him even that weakness, for he had handed me a key" – he paused and chuckled to himself – "and all I had to do was find the door it would open!"

I too laughed at this topsy-turvy reflection, though Melichior's momentary laughter had already frozen on his lips, and he was once again sinking into introspection, ready to go on with this excavation of his own soul.

"And what was this key?" I ventured to ask; but he waved my question aside with a flick of his fingers.

"Iraklitos, the philosopher, spoke of the river and the water, you will remember, and insofar as he was concerned with the aspects of time and singularity he was, of course, right. And yet, in the end, his observation is curiously irrelevant, I find, for the water of the river, the water of any river, of every river, at any time in any place, is always in the process of becoming the water of the Great Sea, which is its own time, both affirmation and negation of the partial being the river once was. Thus, in its end, quite contrary to his conclusions, every river is the same river always" – and he repeated the sentence in Greek to give it point, almost (it crossed my mind) as if suspecting the philosopher himself might be listening, and would thus recognise, in his own language, his own folly.

I was almost as much taken with Melichior's manner of speech as with its thoughtful content; his tone mellifluous, its delivery quiet and modulated, punctuated with so many necessary asides, like listening to a bard reciting a lay or an idyll.

And then I heard how even while becoming one of the most powerful men in the province – which he did when still comparatively young – the ambition to do so, indeed all such ambition, had already deserted him – like water spilled on sand, he said. It was all so effortless, and without point, yet perhaps necessary in its way, for had he not arrived early at that false summit – as he called it – he might never have seen how arid, drab and barren were the valleys and upland pathways by which he had ascended.

This reflection, I own, gave me pause for thought,

coming as it did in the midst of my own disquieting circumstances.

But being there, Melichior was saying, had its value, though not any value he had previously ascribed to it – being there, he saw, as it were… far off, other peaks to climb, though very different, for their summits were invisible, being shrouded in cloud and mist.

And then came something that puzzled me long after he had ceased speaking, like a conundrum: "I knew that the all I already possessed was still nothing and that what I should thenceforth seek also seemed nothing, but that having once found it, it would be all." And, as if that were not in itself sufficient to stretch a mind to the creaking limits of its understanding, the Magus still in him concluded: "But this nothing I possessed and the nothing I would seek must in some way be linked… for the invisible summit could only be approached by way of the visible mountain."

I own that by then I was quite unsure of what all these mountains might be! Substance or figures of something I had not quite grasped. I determined to listen more attentively.

The Judean book was full of mountains, right back to the first mountain, and it was the coincidences in the many stories relating to our origins, of their Noah and our Uta-Napishtim, which had drawn Melichior far into the northern ranges, to Elburz, Nisir and Ararat. He was nearly six years away; at first, not sure what he was there for, later aware that he was still seeking something tangible – remains of the ark? Other signs of the deluge? The Golden Simurgh? Something… anything… which might connect him with the felt truths he had encountered in the writings of the Judeans and of our own ancient seers. But he had found nothing that signified and had returned to Ninevah, perplexed and despondent. Again, after some little time had elapsed, he took to reading those Judean scriptures over again, scrutinising them minutely, looking for the vital correspondences he was convinced he had hitherto failed to notice. But yet again, he had found none.

After a long silence, which, though I was tempted, I did not dare intrude upon with my welling queries, he said: "I do not know how or whence came the intuition, which grew steadily into my mind, that the people and places and things I had sought so diligently, were in themselves probably of little consequence, for they were only a language, moreover, a language whose names belonged almost entirely to the past. And I began to read with new eyes, aware for the first time that it was today's language and tomorrow's which must concern me. And yet, it was that language of the past which, in its way, had finally told me what it was I so badly needed to find, though not in any detail, you understand, but in its... kind.

Although he had named nothing precisely, I felt that I understood something of what he was telling me, of where he was leading. And what followed confirmed me in my belief, even though its words still remained, for a while longer, beyond my reach.

"I had been so obsessed with identifying similarities, correspondences, within the – as it were –

individual words of those two languages... and of words, like places, we tend to make shrines – that the living, all-embracing connection between them had escaped me. Those words – by which, of course, I mean events – whenever for a brief moment the clouds and mist opened to give me a glimpse of the veiled summit – those words signified always a break in the chain, a seeming error, a denial of the pattern long established. Not correspondence then, but the rare or even, indeed especially, the unique or the impossible event, when that which is not subject to time and its attendant laws suddenly bursts in upon time, like a spear of moonlight suddenly shafting through an opening in the clouds on the darkest night.

For me, from the moment of that realisation, the search was over, or rather, was suspended, for all I could do was wait and hope that when the word was spoken I should know it for what it was. And so I have waited, almost seven years, often wondering if it would come at all in my lifetime."

He fell silent and the longer the silence deepened

the more impatient I became for some resolution – for I assumed that after this long narration it must be in the offing.

Coming back to himself he smiled, inwardly almost, that smile I came to know so well in the ensuing weeks, a twinkling smile, mischievous almost, before declaring: "I need not have feared, for when it did come it was clearly spoken. Indeed, had my understanding been more profound – I mean, of what I had by this time read so often I could recite it from memory – I should have known what that word was going to be."

Suddenly, he broke off again and called for refreshment with a clapping of hands. He was seemingly in no hurry to come to what I assumed must be his final revelation. I felt I could not deny him that right and that pleasure, for whatever it was he was perhaps entitled to delay his triumph a little longer... and whatever spiritual edification he believed it would serve. His search, after all, had been long and patient and had been made at a cost of considerable discomfort and self-sacrifice. And yet, I found myself thinking, was this not too a kind of pride, such as he had himself gently derided in the words of the unnamed Judean prophet?

When we had finished our wine and the goblets had been removed, perhaps sensing my impatience, he quickly resumed and concluded his narration.

"This star," he began – as indeed I had already surmised he must begin – "this star which, 'in a manner of speaking' (and I did not miss his gentle irony) you admit you are following. What do you know of it?"

Briefly, because interpreting his question as yet further delay, I told him what I had heard in the tavern and earlier from the village, but did not speak of my own first sight of it, nor of the change in destination it had suddenly imposed upon me, without my understanding how or why.

Yet still he would not be satisfied, and in the end, so as to avoid further delay, I was forced to confess the full effect the star had had upon my life and the lives of those who were then bound to me. He nodded, fell silent a moment, then asked, "Does it not seem strange to you that when the whole world either flees from this star or stands still transfixed by fear, that you alone should be following it?"

His observation took me by surprise, and yet I shrugged my shoulders, unable to offer any answer, for hitherto I had not given the matter even a moment's thought. I had acted, I said, on impulse.

"What I mean," he said, leaning forward, carefully scrutinising my face, "is this. Did you choose to follow it… or were you chosen?"

The bluntness of his question threw me into some consternation, but before I could even begin to formulate my response he had overridden his question with another: "Tell me," he said, with the same intensity as before, "have you any idea where you are going or what you will find when you get there?"

I shook my head, feeling foolish, like an erring schoolboy. "No," I admitted, "none at all. I am going… wherever the star leads." And so as to dispel my earlier fiction I added, "And, as I think you rightly surmise, I have no other business in Jerusalem."

At this he smiled his wrinkling smile. "You may well be surprised where it leads. But let me tell you this. It was foretold many, many lives of men past that this star would arise and would announce the birth of the greatest being who has ever lived upon this earth; one who would redeem the world... Are you prepared for this?"

My laughter would not be contained. "If it is to happen then it will happen, regardless of my state of mind," I answered. "But your words suggest that you know already where we are heading. Is it not to Jerusalem, then?"

"Not finally, no. A little way beyond to the small town of Bethlehem. And if I have understood aright, there will indeed be a royal birth, of the One, the Word, a Pure Language; they say 'He shall be great unto the ends of the Earth' and that 'this Man shall be our Peace.'"

Whereupon he began speaking wholly from

memory, what I took to be a long recitation from his learning of the writings of his Judeans, and as I listened intently to the words he spoke, to my disappointment I gradually came to the view that these prophecies, by which he had seemed to set such great store, were no different from any others I had heard, being at one and the same time too general and too local. And when at last he had finished, I looked up at him, surprised and not a little disarmed, seeing him shaking his head slowly from side to side and nodding, almost ruefully.

"And can you believe all this... rigmarole," I asked him, "which is too vague to be anything but wishful thinking and too specific to be anything but petty...?" But he cut short my protestations.

"I neither believe nor disbelieve, I merely hope. I see possibilities which may be probabilities, and I hope. Perhaps in the next few days we shall have the good fortune to recognise certain coincidences – I mean between what was written and what comes to pass. This I do know, however many coincidences we do observe, they will never be sufficient, for tomorrow always brings new doubts which, in their turn, breed new hopes, and yesterday's language can no longer contain them."

He paused, yet again, perhaps in order that I give his words their proper weight and consideration. But when he spoke once more it was to cast some small doubt on the validity even of that utterance.

"But perhaps we should beware the tyranny of words, for often they seem to free us from darkness only to imprison us anew in half-light."

I considered this proposition for a moment or two but found I could neither gainsay nor endorse it out of my own experience and with that realisation I merely shrugged and waited for him to go on.

"What you have just heard is yesterday's language expressing tomorrow's fears and aspirations, and it fails, frankly, it fails. Yet, on reflection, perhaps we should learn something after all – from the philosopher's rivers, I mean. They find their truth in a final unity: maybe it will be the same with all these different words. Here and there, now and then do not really matter overmuch. Each man finds his own truth or not in his own peculiar way. Is that not so?

The names he gives to it are ultimately of little significance, for they are all names thrown up by circumstance – a street, a mountain, a garden or even a desert; the time of day or night; whether it is raining, whether he looks right or left or straight ahead – but having found his truth let him then not mistake the name for the substance, for in time the name will most surely deny the substance and bring him or those who come after him back to folly and despair."

Here, I had to confess my utter bewilderment. I could not follow the thread of his argument, which was too... abstract, too... abstruse, much less have any inkling of the goal towards which it supposedly moved. But he dismissed my discomfiture with that same slight movement of his hand I had noted earlier. He went on with what I took to be an illustration of his mystifying argument, though I could not be sure that it was so.

"Many times in my life have I taken delight in sitting

by the pool in my garden, looking down into its cool, crystal waters, seeing the fish dart or glide in and out of stones, green stalks and flashing sunlight. And often, as I have watched, I have thought how that pool must be all in all to them, for apart from the startling plunge of the frog at midnight, the rare spattering of raindrops, the rippling breeze, an infrequent human hand, they can have no conception of the vastness all about them. And so it is with us. Our little encompassed world is partial, and the one partiality forever leads to the other, which is ignorance, arrogance and alas, our constant undoing."

At that, he held out both his hands, palms turned upwards, fingers splayed wide apart, in a gesture which betokened the tragic simplicity of it all. "Thus it is," he said – and his face, I saw, now wore a frown – "that whenever I hear the great king speak, the great minister, the great doctor, or indeed the shopkeeper or taverner or tapster, each pronouncing his iron law, formulated in the ooze among his own stones and sedges, I pity the man and I cringe for the world."

He sat back then and gazed into the vast distances

beyond anything our lived experience can encompass.

It was clear that for the moment, at least, he had no intention of saying anything more. He rose to his feet, clapped his hands, and when the servant appeared requested that yet more cushions and a cover be brought for my use; and almost as an afterthought, he turned to me, offering his hospitality and suggesting that we now take our rest and resume our journey, and our talk, after sundown.

I am standing in a river and a strange, impenetrable mist has come down.

The water is already above my knees. I do not know where to make my next move, for I cannot tell which is the way forward or which the way back. I try to see which way the river is flowing but with the curling mist it is impossible to tell. Either I must stand and wait or take a step which, in order that it shall not lose its meaning – its rejection of the other choice, that is – must needs be followed by another and another, until I reach dry land – or drown.

Contemplating this problem, I realise that in this moment (which is endless) I have no other being outside this one dilemma, neither the past, which I can no longer see, nor the future which I can no longer see, nor the river's future nor the river's past. I have lost the sense of action. The river is dammed within me, no longer co-mingling with that which is all about me; I am but am no longer; suspended between then and after, there and yonder, in an eternal now.

In this time which is timeless, nothing I have ever known can help me, least of all, it seems, that knowledge taken from the Ephesian. To take one step would be to step outside reason into fear; reason tells me to stand still and not enter the fear which is all around me; yet, if I follow the counsel of reason, what is my reason if I stand there for ever?

But I am wrong; the river I supposed pent-up within me, my being, is fast dissolving into the shrouding and the empty waters. Forever. Forever. And forever. But I am wrong again. With unseen cause and fathomless motive the unending is suddenly ended.

The mist eddies and tears. Rents like ragged windows are opening all about me and I peer through them into weak sunlight. On the one hand, a caravan, which I instantly perceive to be our own, moving slowly away from the river, gone away backward, when my instinct tells me it should be approaching. I shout and wave frantically through the distorting window, but they do not look back. And on the other hand, a curious archway, decked with roses, through which I see another identical archway, also covered in roses, then another and another until they merge into mist… and my servant is shaking me and another man, whom I do not recognise, stands near, cup in hand. My servant is telling me it is almost nightfall and we must prepare to resume our journey.

There seems to be no end to it. I have long lost count of the days and the nights; no longer a mere step or two along the way between oblivion and oblivion, but by now become the whole of that journey, I sometimes believe. And yet, even as I think it, standing in the doorway of the tent, shielding my eyes from the sun's blinding glare, I am drawn to the sudden sparse scrubland, here and there patches of wiry grass, pale shadows stretching over the sand, not noticed yesterday, certainly not there the day before. And the land slips away on all sides. For the first time in that endless time nothing ahead but the gentle downward slope, disappearing eventually into a distant haze.

Then the slope quickens and after a little while more plunges into a microscopic valley, far below, a thread of silver sunlight silking through it. All day long we toil down the rocky slopes, following our goats, keeping tight rein on our asses and camels, afraid lest they wander too near the brink and in stumbling over, carry us or our precious provisions with them.

Strange how I cannot remember when the last snow had yielded to the temperate upward-wafting current. But it no longer lies in the shadow of overhanging rocks or cowers in the deeper fissures.

We come down gradually into trees and catch the

scent of pine and juniper on the freshening breeze. A freshet bubbles out from the rock at our feet and we kneel to drink from it, reverently almost, splashing its crystal waters up into our grimy faces before dipping our dust-filled heads into its breath-snatching pools. For a brief moment, magus, minister, soldier and drover are become the same delighted children, the warm sun on our backs, icy water running in rivulets down our laughing cheeks, the wilderness now behind us. And as we move off, knowing full well how that moment will be a part of all future sadness, I stop and glance back at my trembling image in the water. But even as I turn, a sudden breeze gusts across its surface and I am gone.

Does my image go before me then, Ephesian, to where all the waters meet?

Some little time after dusk has closed about us, we see the river clearly, just a little way ahead, the early moon dancing in its waters. Here we make our camp, delaying our crossing till the morning, lighter at heart than any of us has been – in my own case, since long before I stole away to cross a greater river, in another distant dawn.

When our camp is already settling for the night, I wander down to the water's edge, half-intent on looking for a crossing-place, though with no particular urgency. The air is crisply cold. Frost is sparkling everywhere. Yet, the kniving wind, which was ever with us in our nocturnal trekking from the east, has mercifully disdained to pursue us from his lair, up on the plateau.

A little way along the river bank, at a place where the trees reach down almost to the water's edge, all at once I find I have entered into a deep silence, like a thicket, and I stop, feeling it pressing in upon me, gently drawing me further and further into itself. Nothing stirs, not a breeze, not a breath, and I have the sensation that the world of things is gently withdrawing, stealing away, and with it all clamour, all cares, time itself, as though resigned to giving me up.

Water laps softly, once, twice, against the low-lying

rocks along a sandy spur over to my left, recalling me, and I walk slowly out along it, almost to the middle of the river. Turning now, I gaze back towards the trees which are flooded in moonlight, and it is in this moment that I hear a sound which is not the sound of lapping water but a night-call, a night creature, faintly, in the trees.

I seem to glide back along the sand-spit and the sound rounds itself, is softer and more plaintive than it was before. It comes to me then, for I had often heard it in the tranquillity of the garden in that other life, the patient cooing of a dove which, perhaps on waking suddenly, the moonlight deceives into believing that day has already come.

Turning again, to retrace my steps, I notice that the latchet of my shoe has come undone and I stoop to fasten it. And as I kneel, yet again that silence of a little while before wraps itself about me and in an instant, sharp as the frost, I perceive the place and significance of all things as though I have soared far above them; yet they have no place in words. And I continue to kneel, afraid lest the slightest movement of my encumbered being jolts time into motion and destroys forever this floating sensation of perfect poise and harmony. If I should never rise and leave this spot I must surely come face to face with whatever is eternal.

Yet I do rise, and in rising lift my eyes to the cloudless night sky, the myriad stars stretching endlessly throughout all that vastness, seeking the one star. And it is there, a great outpouring of light, almost directly overhead.

But it is no longer moving.

It no longer moves.

I blink, turn my eyes away, then back again, close them and open them again, but it moves no longer.

Perplexed, amazed, I hurry back to the tents, intending to wake Melichior, but as I stumble back into the circle defined by the flickering fire, I find him seated outside the great tent, and at my approach he raises his hand in sign of welcome: "I see by your haste that you too have made the same discovery. But it should not surprise us, for how else could a wandering star point us to the place, except by ceasing to wander?"

"It must be over Jerusalem, surely..." I begin to say, but I see him shake his head. "No, not Jerusalem. It has to be Bethlehem, just away to the south. The coincidence it too great for it to fail now."

Is this – whatever it signifies – I wondered later in my bed, awaiting sleep that would not claim me, what Melichior had long been searching for? An area or phase – it was difficult to know how to call it – in which the laws, the very rhythms of the natural world by which men had ever lived and defined their own limits, were being loosened or un-phased. And why? Was it indeed to accommodate some event the like of which we had not known before? Whatever it was, it seemed so strangely to concern me in my own continuing flight.

On the following morning we forded the river and in the distance, yet not too distant, saw we were heading towards a city. Melichior, I knew, was anxious to move on quickly to this place called Bethlehem, but I counselled patience. His men had grown restless of late, quarrels had broken out among them, blood had been drawn, and it was clear from the eager look in the eyes of some that they expected to be set free for a while among whatever delights the city might afford. My servant and the Tarsian brothers – although themselves impatient to come to our journey's end – confirmed my thoughts, and Melichior was persuaded to accede, with a decorous show of magnanimity, to the as yet unspoken demand of his restive soldiers.

There was evident perplexity as we approached and entered in the gate. We had expected the city to be somehow grander, instead of which its walls were broken down in several places and it seemed to lack the bustling prosperity one finds in truly great cities. It was only when I asked our much-travelled Tarsians the way to the fabled temple, with its golden dome, that we learned this was not, after all, Jerusalem, which was still some way off, but the smaller, provincial city of Jericho.

The word spread, and there was disappointment written clearly in the faces of some of the men. Others, however, had gone on ahead and were already beyond recall; be it Jerusalem or Jericho, neither would disappoint them.

The narrow streets were crowded, but even in the central market place the shops and stalls were few, their merchandise poor and common. There were many soldiers in the crowd or standing about in groups, both Roman and Judean, and I wondered whether there was perhaps a garrison in the town or somewhere close at hand. Gradually, however, from taverns and shops and whore-houses, and conversations overheard, we learned that the Romans were conducting a census of all the people in the cities of their birth, which explained at least why many in the streets were so obviously travellers.

This census had apparently been long announced and prepared for. The Roman soldiers had been expected; but not so the Judeans, who had suddenly appeared the day before in great numbers, stopping people in the street, moving from house to house, asking strange questions, rounding up suspected or known troublemakers. There had even been one or two violent clashes between them and the Romans conducting the census, but nobody seemed to know why, nor indeed, what it was they were seeking. And by midday, there was not a single Judean soldier to be found anywhere; they had left as suddenly as they came, and no one, we gathered, was sorry to see the back of them.

After so many days and nights spent sleeping in tents, we decided to avail ourselves of whatever comfort Jericho had to offer and so asked for rooms at several inns, but with all the commotion caused by the census none were to be had anywhere and it was with some disappointment that we had to resign ourselves once more to our tents.

It was while we were inquiring at one of the inns near the city centre that we learnt from the landlord of a similar request made to him about a week before, by the servants of a king, no less! A king? A king! What would a king be doing in a flea-pit like this Jericho? Like ourselves he was a traveller, passing through on his way to find *the* King, but strangely, it transpired, it was not the Judean King Herod he was seeking at all. Like it or not, though, in the end he had been escorted to Herod's palace, in Jerusalem, by a large contingent of the Palace Guard which, it seems, had suddenly arrived at daybreak – just as they had that selfsame morning – and, it was said, surrounded the large encampment of this foreign king, just outside the city on the southern side.

And where had he come from this foreign king? From the east – some said from southern Arabia, others said as far away as India. What was he like? This, the landlord could not tell us for he had not set eyes on him, though judging by the apparel of his servants (not to mention the price they were offering or the money they spent), a great king – indeed, a very great king! No one was sure what had become of him, though later that same day the camp had broken up and his followers had all gone off in the direction of Jerusalem.

You couldn't blame Herod, so large was this foreign king's company. He could be forgiven for fearing marauders or even an invasion… though come to think of it, it hadn't seemed to worry the Romans – not that they cared much anyway, so long as the tribute came in regularly and there wasn't any trouble collecting it.

A glance told me that this intelligence was worrying Melichior, even before he mentioned it, and I thought I knew why. Reluctant to make even this stop in Jericho, he did not wish to be delayed even longer by an enforced visit to Herod. Yet, failure to make the journey to Jerusalem, now that we were so close, would seem at least discourteous, at worst suspicious to a king who was, in any case, reputed to be exceedingly jealous of the little power the Romans had left him.

And thus it was we discussed the problem with the guides and with Melichior's captain, and eventually came to the decision that our best strategy was for us temporarily to disband into several smaller groups, each of which would make its own way to Bethlehem, over the next two days. The captain was immediately dispatched to the eastern gate where our baggage train had been left, so as to organise the groupings and the division of supplies as the men drifted back.

This arrangement had the very great advantage of freeing Melichior and myself to go on with all speed to our destination.

At this point, my servant Rastim reminded me of my promise to the Tarsian brothers who, although their task of droving had ended several days before when the last of our beasts was eaten, had remained with us. In truth, they had long won the respect of all our company with their tireless labour, knowledge of the terrain and wise counsel about the difficulties encountered along the way. But when we found them, already back at the gate helping to mind the pack animals, they would not hear of leaving us yet. Jerusalem? Bethlehem? What did it matter which? And besides, quite apart from our need of their skill – for the area west and south of Jericho was the last fastness of the worst rebels and bandits – they were curious; all this talk; all these rumours… To give up now… at this last stage? Karesh shook his head decidedly. If we would permit it, they would accompany us all the way.

And yet, they were sceptical. Oh yes, they too had noticed that the star had stopped. But this was a land that was full of prophecy – it always had been – in which every new generation, since further back than anyone could remember, had been sure that a Saviour would come, a Deliverer, and it would be they who would be privileged to receive him. Their whole stagnant history had been one of waiting for the future – and you could see why. Look around you. All this desolation. Not just the desert and the barren mountain ranges either, but that town, it stank of poverty and oppression. A downtrodden people perpetually imprisoned by peoples more powerful than themselves; how could they go on if not supported by such dreams? Nevertheless... And Karesh shook his head again, exhaling audibly as he did so, a groan almost. I looked at him intently, waiting, but when he saw me scrutinising him he merely shrugged his shoulders.

"Nevertheless... what?" I persisted.

He seemed about to speak, but checked himself, smiling awkwardly. He began again and checked a second time, becoming suddenly, uncharacteristically, self-conscious. "I drive animals much more easily than words," he said, laughing again, nervously, and then, at first haltingly, began to explain what he had meant.

"Some years ago, we were engaged… my brother and I… as part of a team of drovers, far to the south and east of here, though in a land which greatly resembled this. The drive was hard and long, the springs and water holes scarce, and we lost many of our beasts and our spirits were low. Then suddenly, one morning, after we had already been moving along a valley bottom for what seemed an endless time, with the sun beating down upon us yet again, the team leader called a halt and turning round shouted to us: 'We are come at last, let us move the beasts quickly into the city.' And we all stood and looked about us in bewilderment, surrounded as we were by rock and sand, the rust-red mountains rearing up on either side, a towering cliff face all along the valley bottom over to our right.

We looked from one to another fearing that the rigours of the journey, the merciless sun, had turned the brain of our leader, one of the best drovers we had ever worked with. For in that barren, lifeless spot there was not the slightest trace of human habitation, nor of nature's foison – not a blade of grass, even – it seemed the very domain of death itself.

Seeing that none of us moved, and sensing our perplexity, he came towards us. 'Have none of you ever been here before, then?' Again we looked at each other, wondering what he could mean. And not knowing how to answer some of us shook our heads, others shrugged or just looked down at the sand, but all stayed silent. Then he laughed out loud – a man not normally given to jocularity – and pointing at the sheer cliff face shouted, 'There it is, the great and ancient city of Petra'; and now we really did fear for his sanity."

Melichior, who all the while had stood silently beside me, laughed out loud, startling me. "But of course," he said. "Of course. I understand now. Petra. Why, yes, of course!"

"You see?" said Karesh, "You understand now what it is that makes us want to go on, despite most things we have ever known?"

"Yes. I think I do... and wisely so!" said Melichior.

Karesh turned away then, as if to occupy himself with the preparations for our imminent departure, but I stopped him, taking him by the arm, at the same time looking at Melichior.

"I'm sorry," I said, quite at a loss, "but... I understand nothing."

Both men laughed and Melichior, echoing the words of Karesh's sometime companion, said "Have you never been here before, in Petra?" But before I could answer he went on, "you see, Petra is a city hidden behind a curtain of mountains and can be approached – or so I understand, for I have never been there myself – only through a narrow gully that leads up through the cliff face.

From where they were standing, I imagine, there was nothing to distinguish that vent in the rock from the thousands of others, each one of which, they knew from long experience, ended always in flat, barren rock, confirming time after time after time the iron laws of the nature of this endless wilderness. Where they least expected it… there was the exception." And he looked at Karesh, seeking confirmation, "Am I right…?"

Karesh nodded vigorously.

Melichior turned back towards me, then. "… And they could so easily have missed it, that miraculous contradiction of everything around it. What Karesh is saying, I think" – and he turned again towards our companion – "is that Bethlehem may well hold such another contradiction.

It is, if you like, precisely... the invisible summit and the visible mountain I spoke of, you may remember, on the day of our first meeting."

But having now aligned my thoughts with theirs, it occurred to me that their logic hobbled somewhat, and I said so: "But this contradiction, this broken… link… at Petra, miracle though it seemed… because of the huge contrast between what appeared dead and what was living, was nonetheless… still… all on the plain of the natural. Whereas in Bethlehem, if I have understood what you have many times said, we may well find something that… that is beyond the natural, so that we are not really comparing two like orders of experience… are we?"

Melichior looked suddenly aggrieved and shook his head from side to side, clearly impatient at my reasoning. "The mountain and the summit; the visible and the invisible; the city and the desert, the invisible and the visible. Do not talk to me of orders of experience, my good friend, for in the moment of the visible the summit seems impossible, the city – by Karesh's own admission – the ravings of an addled mind. Yet, the summit and the city are there all the time, they don't suddenly appear from nowhere; the miracle is the discovery of their presence and of their attainability, it is in the adjustment of the mind to a higher threshold of possibility in the moment. And consider. It cannot be other than natural, whatever it is, if it takes place in this world, for how else can this world express itself? The miracle, I tell you, takes place in the mind of man. Invariably. Always."

Of course, I saw the logic in his argument, yet could not free myself from the cloying notion of that antithesis, the natural and the supposedly more than natural that… this Saviour… seemed to be… must be… if the fulfilment of ancient prophecy.

"My dear Balthazar, if you hold fast to those dimensions, you are destined to remain the prisoner of all these dead things." And so saying, he stooped down and picked up a stone and forced me to take it in my hand. "Look! Here is *your* reality. It is nothing. It has nothing. You hold it close, yet it knows you not, neither do you know it. This nature has no nature. Instead of *this* stone, hold on to that idea of Petra, on that firm rock… one can *surely* build."

I admired his dexterity with words but was conscious too that words distil even faster than the breath that utters them. He was right, of course. The stone, the city, the dust, the air, everything, had reality only because I conferred it by naming it and privileging it, but the moment I turned my back… yes, it ceased to be anything at all. Yet the tyranny of things is more potent than that of any empire, for there is no vision that is not shaped by them; a wasting disease of the soul, they destroy us because we love them so and can rarely escape our addiction for them.

We elected to travel once more by night. There was no practicable route to Bethlehem other than the road west to Jerusalem. Hazardous even by day, particularly for the lone traveller, its perils seemed compounded a hundredfold by the shifting darkness. Nonetheless, we conjectured, it was unlikely that the military, either Judean or Roman, would be abroad by night, and our company, though small, was large enough still, and well-armed enough, to see off any but the largest and most determined band of brigands. We sought, in truth, to use the evil reputation of the road itself to protect us, for who would be so foolish as to attempt it at night? And who, therefore, would lose sleep waiting for a prize that was unlikely to come?

Our experience proved us right in taking the risk. Muffling the hooves of our camels and horses, moving in single file and speaking only in whispers, we made unhindered progress and by daybreak had already left the Jerusalem road far behind us.

And yet, there had been a moment of very real fear which left us shaken and not a little perplexed.

It was Kadish, the younger of the Tarsian brothers, who in that moment happened to be at the rear of our column, who first noticed it and came hurrying up to the front, first to his brother, then to us, pointing away into the darkness to the south of the road. There we beheld a red-gold glow behind a high hill, which gradually emerged in silhouette from the darkness as the light rose and in rising, intensified. We all of us stopped to watch it, clustering together, speechless.

Many times in my earlier years I had witnessed the destruction of villages and farms by fire, at night, and though it was this which came at once to my mind I was sure that that light had nothing to do with fire. There was no flickering, no smoke. It seemed to swell gradually and uniformly until it had attained its full power. It hung over the hill, brighter than the sun, surely blinding to anyone who had the misfortune to be caught near it. Even we, who were at a great distance, could not bear that glow for more than a few seconds without turning our eyes away. And there it remained for what seemed a very long time until slowly it died back to its original red glow along the hill top before finally dissolving back into darkness.

For some time after the light had vanished we all remained where we were, our eyes fixed on the spot where it had last been – or rather, now, staring into the impenetrable blackness. But it did not come again.

Then a tugging at my harness signalled our new departure, though some came slowly, still looking back, whether afraid or reluctant I could not tell. And when I had caught up with Melichior I sensed he too was deep in thought, and although it was impossible to be sure, he seemed to be smiling.

But then we had to wait awhile, for it quickly became apparent that two of our number were not yet with us. Someone then turned back to fetch them and after some little time came up with Karesh and Kadish, both still glancing back every now and again.

No one had yet broken the silence that had descended upon us after our first gasps of awe and wonder, and strangely, I had the sensation that it was somehow deepening in us and over us, as though we were drowning.

And as we rode on, I searched my memory for some scrap of knowledge or lived experience that might point me towards an explanation of that disturbing phenomenon of light, but I found none.

Just as dawn was starting to dispel the darkness over the distant hills, we turned off the Jerusalem road onto one which, though narrower, was obviously much used, or rather, which bore all the signs of having been recently used by many travellers. It snaked back and forth to avoid the worst of the steep, rocky slope on the right and the deepening ravine over to the left, and once or twice it was impossible to move forward except in single file.

By the time the sun had cleared the mountain tops to the south and east, away beyond the gleaming waters of where Melichior said must lie the Sea of Salt, we had come out into more open country and some little way ahead could see the smoke rising from a village which was already bustling about its daily business. Soon, people began to pass us going in the direction whence we had come, shepherds and farmers in the main, but also longer travellers off to an early start; and it was then I remembered the census.

We decided to pass right through the village, to tether our animals beneath the trees we could see at the farther end, and then return on foot in search of food, for all of us were hungry and ready to break our fast.

Our talk, now, was all of the strange light we had witnessed in the darkest hours of the night. And yet it was desultory, some of our company seeming impatient with it, as though not wanting to talk of it at all, as something become already private and inward. Melichior confessed himself baffled; he had never known such a light before, nor heard of one, but the

67

light, he reminded me, was itself merely an effect, however wonderful, and if the effect stirred no memories in any of us, what of its cause?

He leaned over to me.

"I remember reading in those Judean scriptures something like: 'And there shall come a light out of Israel' – but I had never thought to interpret that prophecy in a literal sense; and now it would seem too opportunistic." He laughed, I remember, perhaps at his own presumed folly, but by then I had ceased almost to heed his words for as we walked along something else had half caught my attention and was pulling at my thoughts.

In the moments which followed I easily accepted my own half-surmised explanation that my eyes and my mind, focused as they were on Melichior, had been somehow divided by a trick of the light, an image distorted because squeezed into the corner of my eye as we strolled slowly along the middle of the street. The image intruded, became curiosity, drove out concentration, leaving barely the shell of politeness, so that as soon as Melichior paused in his reflections, I touched his arm.

"Wait a moment!" I said, and hurried back twenty or so paces to the open door and stood looking in.

Melichior, whose own curiosity had been aroused by my unusual behaviour, followed and stood by my side. "What is it? What have you seen?"

And in truth, I could not say in that moment what I had seen, for my mind had not yet fastened sufficiently on the image held by my mind's eye, but certainly, what I had seen was something other than the young girl whom I now beheld bending over a great wooden ewer, just inside the door, washing her long, raven-black hair. But even as we stood and regarded her, still oblivious as she was of our presence, a sharp, not unpleasant smell reached our nostrils.

"What is it?" I asked Melichior, as we turned away into the street, "It is quite new to me, I think."

He smiled his twinkling smile as he began to answer. "We have no word for it that I know of, but it is an ointment which the Greeks call *Narthou Stakis*. It is made from a plant which bears the same name."

"And what are its uses?" I urged, leaving the girl to her innocent task.

"It is mainly used as a balm, I believe, though in some places, I have heard tell, it is also used in the preparation of the dead for the sepulchre."

For some reason I could not explain, this last intelligence brought me back sharply to that original image, which had occasioned my return, suspended now in my mind's eye, awaiting understanding, like a dream fading.

The girl had not been washing her hair. There had been a tall, thin man with her, dressed in the coarse white robe which I had already learned was common in those parts. He had been standing looking down at her, his hand, I am almost certain, resting gently on her head, while she, and this was the strange thing, that which had compelled me, seemed to be wiping his feet with her hair. But that could not be, surely. Perhaps the long stream of early sunlight, with its dancing motes and beams, through the open doorway, and the girl's glistening hair spread over the tub, had somehow tricked my inattentive eye.

Yet this explanation felt somehow incomplete, for of all possible things, illusion or not, why that one?

I stopped and looked back.

The girl had come out of the house now and was busy drying her hair with a towel, in the sun. Then she suddenly became aware, as one does, that she was being watched. She lowered her towel and smiled shyly. I smiled back and raised my hand in salutation, and she made as if to return to her task after a momentary hesitation. Encouraged, I took a step or two towards her and shouted, "The man – the man in the white robe – Is he ... where did he go?"

Perhaps the distance was already too great, or maybe she simply did not understand my words. Her brow puckered into a frown, her head tilted slightly to one side like a bird's, then her bewilderment was transformed into her shy, modest smile; she shrugged and, it seemed, shook her head before she turned away and went back inside the house.

Some little while after we had eaten, we returned to our tethered beasts by the same way and I looked for her again, but I did not see her. As we waited for one of Melichior's soldiers to adjust his saddle straps, I sat gazing back up the street, but she did not reappear. Then, when all was ready, we rode away from the village, whose name I never knew.

We reached Bethlehem a little before noon that same day.

Shortly after leaving the girl's village we had rejoined a wider road, the one that lies directly between Bethlehem and Jerusalem. There were people everywhere, moving in both directions, and we even had to step off the road, at one point, to let a detachment of Roman soldiers pass.

The day, which had started brightly, was now overcast and every now and again a sudden gust of wind would stir up the dust and set it whirling about us and we were obliged to keep our faces covered for much of the time, so conversation was sparse. The moment we had joined the bigger road, Bethlehem had been visible, or rather, its low-lying silhouette could just be made out against the coppery, cloud-filled sky, probably nearer, we surmised, than it appeared to be. That so many people could apparently have business in a place of its size amazed us, until yet again, when the soldiers passed, Melichior remembered that, as the home of one of the historically important families of Judea, it too must be one of the census points.

And once more, as in Jericho, we gave up all hope of finding beds and decided to pitch our tents beside the dusty road beneath the town. Besides, it would make things easier for the rest of our company to find us, as their different groups came to the town over the next day or so.

Even here, however, we found that many had come before us with the same idea; a veritable town of tents and makeshift shelters had sprung up and the traders had quickly come down from the town with their vegetables, bread, homespuns and water, bent on ensuring that their short-lived good fortune should profit them to the full.

Once our tents were in place, we decided, we would rest for several hours before going on up into the town. All of us were weary, but especially Melichior, I noted, and not even his burning desire to put the truth of his scriptures to the test – "the word become flesh," as he so quaintly put it – could stir him.

As the rest of us struggled to raise the big tent, in the gusting wind, Melichior sat on one of the packs unloaded from the camels, seeming to doze, his eyes already closed. But he was not asleep, for it was he who eventually pointed to the procession of camels, horses and asses which came slowly, majestically, wending its way along the road we had lately traversed ourselves. Our curiosity aroused, we ceased from our labours and turned to watch them pass. We knew at once it must be someone of great importance, for the main caravan was flanked on either side by soldiers, Judeans, whose uniforms we immediately recognised from the day before.

As they drew level with us, many of the people who were already encamped on the other side of the road, and just a little nearer to the town than we were ourselves, flocked to the roadside, shouting and waving excitedly, seemingly recognising this personage now clearly visible to us, almost at the head of the column, astride a pure white stallion. I found myself wondering whether this might be no less a personage than Herod himself.

Then the procession stopped.

The captain of the contingent of Judean soldiers dismounted, and passing the reins of his horse to a soldier, who rode a little way behind him, walked back towards the man on the stallion. A few paces away from him he paused, made a sign of obeisance, was raised by a movement of the prince's hand (for such, at very least, I took him to be) and came then right up to him. They conversed for a moment or two before the captain returned to his horse, mounted, and raising his hand, rode slowly down the flanking column on the farther side. And as he passed, each mounted soldier turned his horse and followed, and those on our side of the road took their lead from those on the other side until all came together a little beyond the rear of the stationary caravan, and cantered off in a cloud of dust, towards Jerusalem.

When the soldiers were gone the people at the roadside rushed forward to mingle with those from the already disintegrating caravan, and the whole crowd of them headed off together towards the circle of tents over on the other side. We too returned to our task, and only with great difficulty – for we felt our lack of numbers – finally succeeded in raising our tent. Whereupon Melichior and I retired immediately to rest, leaving our people to prepare their own less unwieldy shelters and to attend to their other tasks.

I awoke suddenly, not knowing where I was, and it was already almost dark. I sensed rather than saw that I was alone. Rising from my cushions, I groped my way outside and immediately found Rastim. Melichior, it seemed, had not slept at all and had thus quietly answered a summons to visit the man whom we had seen arriving on the white stallion, earlier in the afternoon. He had been gone several hours already, but had sent instructions that when I awoke I should be apprised of his whereabouts and be invited to join him, if I wished to do so.

Curious to know more about the identity, provenance and presence of the lordly stranger who travelled with so numerous a train, I set out towards the shadowy tents beyond the now almost deserted road, accompanied by two of Melichior's guard.

My arrival was clearly expected, for without ceremony I was ushered into a tent which, I saw at a glance, was greater and more sumptuous in its trappings than even Melichior's, and where I found the dark, sharp-featured stranger and my friend deep in conversation, barely pausing to wave me to the cushions that had apparently been laid there in preparation for my coming.

The stranger – who was younger than I had imagined him to be – was speaking earnestly, but quietly and, I soon perceived, in the language of the eastern lands which, if it shares many words with our own tongue, also possesses many others that were then unknown to me. As a consequence, and because I had wandered into the middle of a conversation which had already run for several hours, I had great difficulty in following much of what he said. He seemed to be speaking about eyes which never for one moment left him (or someone) as he moved about a room. Then he seemed to change direction, and I realised that I had missed some vital thread, for he spoke about an intuition which was surer and more vital than any knowledge born of, or defined by, rationality or lived experience.

Frustratingly, I could not fathom the point out of the fragments in my mind. I am not sure what, if anything, I had expected to find in making my visit to the tent, but I am certain I had not anticipated that almost total incomprehension, those words I could not come to grips with.

Then came something else I could not follow, then

something (I think) about the transmigration of souls – but, with mounting impatience, I again failed to catch the connections which he must have made.

I watched Melichior's face intently, in the hope that his expression might betray some further hint as to the subject of their discourse, but apart from his usual intensity and an air of tolerance or even agreement I found little to assist me. And yet, there was something; something heavy, sombre even, about the atmosphere vacated by those final words.

The silence settled into sadness and reflection and I felt myself, I then realised, an intruder upon some intensely private grief, without having the least notion of what it was, and my embarrassment at being there intensified the longer the silence lasted, becoming almost unbearable.

Melichior, who was always alive to the slightest shift in emotion and atmosphere, after waiting for what felt to be an endless time in which the silence washed over us, wave upon wave, seeming to drown all thought, spoke gently – to me, ostensibly, but with the real purpose of coaxing our younger host away from his hopeless contemplation of what must have been a deeply-felt grief.

"His Majesty, King Gathaspah, has newly come from visiting King Herod in Jerusalem, and so concerned was the latter for his safety in these troubled parts and times he even dispatched a company of his soldiers to bring him to Bethlehem – as indeed he had so kindly sent others to bring him to Jerusalem from Jericho, several days before."

His gently ironical smile, to which I had grown accustomed, flickered again as he spoke, knowing as he did that I had already heard another version of those earlier events, in Jericho.

Gathaspah looked up and he too smiled at Melichior's over-tactful gloss on Herod's solicitude. "Almost, we were prisoners, if generously entertained," he explained. "Herod is without doubt a man extremely worried by virtue of certain rumours which have reached him about the coming of a Deliverer"; some even say a fulfilment of the ancient scriptures of these lands. Yet he affects humility and a desire to kneel at this new king's feet and to beg him to rid this land of the Roman scourge. In truth, if what I have seen and heard in Jerusalem these past five days is typical of what people must endure under Herod, then I judge that it is only the presence of the Romans that stands between them and complete disintegration into anarchy."

At this new turn in the conversation, I thankfully suddenly found myself on a much firmer footing, able to follow with greater ease – though even so, the king's strange accentuation of certain words was still cause of occasional, momentary confusion.

"This wily king," he continued, "has charged *me* with the task of seeking out this Deliverer and bringing him news so that he too might 'follow and fall at his feet in homage and abject humility'. He has also, at the same time, as a precaution perhaps, sought to buy the loyalty of two of my captains, who are to keep him informed of my doings and my inquiries in the meantime." He shook his head, his face contorting into a grimace that was not quite a smile. "Who would be so foolish as to trust such a man or become caught up in the viscous thread of his intrigues? When the time comes, many though we are, we shall slip away so silently and so completely into the dead lands that Herod's people will not find us, though they turn over each stone or sift through every handful of sand."

His voice was soft but with a curious lilt to it, which became more pronounced when he spoke with feeling; yet even so it seemed to impose a silence, and not just because one required it to catch his words, rather did it seem to come from within, a quiet authority which expected to be heard.

"Shall we take a little refreshment, then go and see whether whatever it is we are here for awaits us up in the town?" he proposed.

Melichior turned towards me, raising his eyebrows in question. I sensed King Gathaspah's gaze upon me also, and all at once for no reason that was apparent, this decision had seemingly become mine.

"I, at least, am already well rested after our gruelling

journey, and would indeed welcome a visit to the town, but what of you? Are you not still exhausted?" And though I addressed my question to them both my concern was chiefly for Melichior rather than the much younger man.

Melichior, interpreting the wish of the king and submitting to his own burning curiosity, replied jestingly, "Youth and age have little time for sleep, good Balthazar, it is the years in between which seize every opportunity of renouncing here and now for dreams of before and after – as you must know."

The little town is overwhelmed. Its few, narrow, ill-lit streets jammed almost to a standstill, the aimless crowds milling to and fro, unable to find even the commonest city amusements here, the two or three inns being small and the few traders ill-equipped to provide for any but the most basic needs. This chaos seems an unlikely setting for anything of lasting significance; in two or three days at the most Bethlehem will have become once more what it has probably always been, and in two or three weeks no one there will give a thought to this brief moment in which the whole world – or so it must seem – has descended upon it.

Of the three of us, I admit, I was the least prepared. I had neither the knowledge nor the capacity for belief that my companions displayed; at most, a vague curiosity and, by then, a deep attachment to Melichior.

What we are there for and what form it will take, if at all, I hardly know. There has been much talk of a king, a Deliverer, especially during these past few hours, but why would a king want...? But then I think of Gathaspah and reformulate my incredulity. Is it likely that not one, but two kings might find themselves on the same day in this place of no significance, between Jerusalem and the vast wilderness of Sinai and Arabia, and if so, for what purpose, where neither the one nor the other has any authority? – as the occasional pairs or small groups of Roman soldiers continually remind us.

I remember, as we reached the far end of this town

– or village, as it more properly was – feeling suddenly despondent, not so much, I think, for myself but for Melichior, who had come so far, already advanced in years, driven on by some deep, inner need, and arriving here where the feeble rush lamps set at each door peter out, to stand blinking into the darkness beyond. It was for me the worst moment of our whole journey, the abyss we all suspect and fear lies just beneath whatever solidity and certainty even our best moments contrive.

I think the others must have felt something of this also, though neither of them spoke. They stood there, a little apart, a little way beyond where I had stopped, staring into the blackness, a sudden breeze tugging at their robes.

At length, Gathaspah turned and spoke to Melichior, but I did not catch his words. We began then to pick our way once more back through the slowly eddying multitude that paralysed the middle part of the town.

Our conversation had lapsed, in part because the continual hubbub all about us made it difficult to communicate without raising our voices in a way to which none of us was accustomed, and also, I was sure, because of an inner tension which gradually tightened as slowly we saw ourselves once more nearing the bottom gate by which we had entered.

It was a disappointment. But, for the present at least, there was nothing to keep us there.

But then the crowd parted to make way for two soldiers and their wide-eyed, helpless prisoner, still clutching the small loaf for the theft of which, I presumed, he had been taken.

At another point, a woman fell down in a fit, foaming and twitching on the ground, and those about her drew back and stared in fascinated horror, and no one went forward to help her, convinced as they all were (as I later discovered) that she was being ravished by the devil before their very eyes! Melichior pushed his way forward angrily, bent down beside her and, motioning us to assist him, began to turn her onto her side, explaining that it was to prevent her from swallowing her tongue and choking to death, as he had once seen happen to a child in the throes of a similar convulsion. I saw too that he knotted the woman's shawl and thrust the knotted end between her lips, at the same time wiping away the blood-tinted froth which had gathered at the corners of her mouth.

At length, the uncontrolled shaking and moaning subsided and Melichior called for water, and when it was not immediately brought to him he turned and pointed at a burly shepherd, leaning on his staff, and ordered him to fetch water at once. Meekly, if sullenly, the man obeyed, though hastily placing the vessel a few paces from us before making off into the anonymity of the crowd. We raised the woman's head and shoulders, at Melichior's request, propping her up against the small bundle of garments people round about said was her own. When, at last, she opened her eyes, Melichior helped her drink, and it was only then that a man and woman came forward, somewhat shamefacedly, to help her; her sister and her sister's husband. They appeared confused and ashamed, but Melichior explained to them about their sister's affliction, that it was caused by natural imbalances or deficiencies and not by supernatural intervention of any sort. Patiently, he also demonstrated to them what they must do should the woman ever again be seized by a similar attack.

When we made to leave, the crowd hurriedly drew aside, some, I noticed, even flattening themselves against the walls of the houses on the other side of the narrow street, clearly afraid lest we should touch them.

"Make way for the physician!" someone shouted nervously; but such incitements proved unnecessary, though I could not help wondering with some amusement, how many had been injured in their haste to get well beyond the reach of this particular 'physician'. I was amazed, given the intensity of the throng, that so much space could still be made available!

And so it is we pass on into a street which crosses the main thoroughfare, yet I realise, even as the crowd closes behind us, that it is not a street at all but a long, inn yard, a lantern swinging gently from a post at an open stable door and a fainter glow coming from within. I check and turn back, thinking that my friends will do the same, but when I turn to speak I see, to my surprise, that they have gone on and are just now passing in through the door, silhouetted for a brief moment before they disappear inside. I wait a while for them to come out again, but then, not seeing them, go forward, a shade irritated at the absurdity, and enter into the byre.

I am quite unprepared for what I find there. Instead of coming face to face with my companions, their momentary curiosity satisfied by disappointment, I see at once that the place is full of people, standing four or five deep, their backs towards the door, staring at something which, as yet, I cannot see. Nor do I catch sight of my friends, for – as I am eventually to discover – they have eased their way to the front, despite the protestations of those who have got there before them. Standing on tiptoes, leaning lightly for support on the shoulders of the man in front of me, craning my neck, I am just able to see what has drawn this crowd into the stable. A peasant girl of no more than sixteen or seventeen years is sitting on a bale of straw, a lamp flickering behind her, and even as I take in this unexpected scene it crosses my mind that she is either a mad girl on show for entertainment or simply whoring, though perhaps not a professional, maybe just down from Jerusalem for the night, peddling her favours in the hay, trying to make a little extra money while the opportunity lasts.

But almost at once I know I am wrong. She is bending down and touching something I cannot see in the manger beside her, and even as I watch she raises her head, gently brushing a strand of hair, which has escaped her austere coiffure, back from her face, and it is her face, but also something rare in her being, transmitted in her movements, which tells me she is neither insane nor of easy virtue. Entirely wrapt in her own gentle being, her movements precise but not self-conscious, she barely seems to notice our gaping presence, for whatever this scene is it is not spectacle, rather something intense and private.

It is that face, glimpsed in that instant, that lives again now in my mind's eye, as I have seen it countless times since in the intervening years, with its almost vacant smile, here but never really among us, like a cooling breeze in the heat of the night, felt, real, immediate, yet departing, insubstantial, a transposition that leaves us dissatisfied, longing, never quite believing in this world of appearances that seeks in vain to hold it to itself and its perpetual fading.

Of course, none of this belonged with that moment. It is, rather, a distillation of it over long years, the vital communication that grows out of immeasurable silence.

In that moment, caught by that look, I felt only shame, for myself and for my fellow human-beings who had drifted in out of boredom or curiosity to intrude on that intimate joy and misfortune – for such I then took it to be – of that serene, young mother. For of course, she was a mother. Yet even now, I cannot decide whether, in that brief interlude in the stable, I saw the child. I suspect not, for I have no recollection of her lifting him up nor did I move any closer, as my friends had done. With that first flush of shame I left and, despite the later entreaties and assurances of Melichior and Gathaspah, could not bring myself to go back there. Since then I have often regretted, yet now I know it does not matter overmuch, for however vital and necessary that tableau, assembled in and for that moment, neither endured nor needed to do so. To have glimpsed it and felt it was enough.

In the days that followed, I listened intently to the long conversations between Melichior and Gathaspah, often reaching far into the night. Each day for several days to come, they went, sometimes together, occasionally each one alone, to talk with the strange couple up at the stable, the child mother and the much older husband, who could so easily have been taken for her father.

In my anxiety not to embarrass or be embarrassed in that very company, it had not occurred to me that I was witnessing the very thing we had come to find. I saw then merely with this world's eyes. It was only gradually, in part through listening to the reasoning and reports of my companions as they returned from their several visits, in part through my own memory (or was it fantasy?) of those few moments in the stable, that the reaction I have already described began to take on another different shape and significance.

Whenever I returned in memory to that experience, I saw, as I was hurriedly departing, through a gap, which for a mere instant had opened up between the tightly packed bodies of the gaping spectators, the kneeling figure of Karesh. In truth, it was only in memory that I saw him, for I know that my thoughts had not encompassed him as I had pushed back through the swirling crowds still occupying the main street. And that kneeling was so clearly an act of supplication, so out of character; a troubling enigma, though later confirmed by Melichior, who had been near him.

For Melichior, patient and subtle questioning of the man (the woman, evidently, remained silent all the while), out of his vast knowledge of the Judaic scriptures and legends, had led him quite logically and easily to the conviction that the centuries' old promises were probably being fulfilled, though the man – in whom he found no guile – had no notion that it was so. There was no knowing what the girl thought for she kept her own counsel. Yet, having arrived at that conviction, he was perplexed about its possible meanings, for future generations, not just for our own – for a child in a manger could become anything, yet in those few days since his birth was merely helplessness, a Deliverer who, as it was soon to turn out, was himself in need of deliverance.

And yet, when all was considered, if this child, as a man, brought nothing different from Alexander or Xerxes or the greatest of all the Pharaohs, even though to a downtrodden race, what value could such deliverance have? For in a twinkling of the eye of time, those who had been raised up would surely be cast down, for such was ever the fashion of history.

In short, having reasoned himself into acceptance

of a prophecy, he could not then reason himself out of its consequences, its seeming banality, and he became irritable, morose, desirous of much more than the reality seemed to offer.

Gathaspah had been silent on returning from that first visit, but – it later emerged – had then returned secretly and alone a second and a third time during that same night and early on the following day, and when some days later, finally pressed by Melichior to say what *he* believed it was they had seen, he amazed us by his answer.

If initially it had been the bearing and mien of that child-mother which had engaged him, as indeed they had been so deeply disturbing to me also, it was not finally that, or indeed anything else about that small family, what they said or even seemed to be, which persuaded him that here was something quite beyond any normal sort of experience. "You see," he said, "what struck me more forcefully than anything else was the strange yet consistent behaviour of the other occupants of the stable."

"Other occupants?" I repeated, suspecting that my own fleeting visit, my almost cursory glance, had not after all told me very much at all.

He stared at us, challenging, impatient. "Do you mean you did not, have not yet noticed them, Melichior?"

The old man shook his head; no, he had not, for his whole preoccupation had been with trying to connect the message of the ancient scriptures with that present moment, a wholly intellectual occupation, he owned, and perhaps for that reason, he granted, wholly inadequate. He cackled dryly at his own thought, that part already revealed and that part only now perhaps dimly perceived, as yet in shadow.

Gathaspah nodded, recognising the concession which was also, in its odd way, an invitation to continue.

"The ass, the oxen, and even – did you really not notice? – the this-year's lambs and calves, the donkey foal, how they stood quite still, never moving all the time we were there and, from wherever they stood, fixed their eyes, as though bewitched, on the manger where the child lay, as if some arcane power held them, binding their poor, simple wills to its own."

Melichior, visibly discomfited, made a vague gesture of incomprehension, of impatience maybe; but Gathaspah smiled and nodded. "Yes, precisely that, that was my persistent response also as I went over and over it, lying awake in the dark. It was not being able to believe what my eyes had seen which drove me back there hours later. When I stole into the stable, the man and woman were sleeping. The lamp was still burning, though a little further off than before. The child's eyes were open, but again it was the animals which commanded my attention, for wherever they stood or lay – and, I swear, their stillness was absolute – their eyes were upon the child, never leaving him for one instant, as though my presence was as yet unnoticed – or without significance. It was the same when I returned a second time, an hour or two later."

Melichior had been standing in the doorway of the tent, staring out across the desert, but now he turned, deep in thought, and came slowly back to the chair near where Gathaspah and I were sitting, and he perched himself on the edge of it, leaning forward, chin resting in his cupped hand. "What you are saying then is that this is no child in the ordinary sense; that this affinity or recognition or whatever it is you have observed in these dumb creatures points to ... ?" – But suddenly he found he could not go on, and in his frustration he jumped to his feet, striding back and forth in front of us, struggling to force unwilling words to his purpose.

Finally, Gathaspah came to his aid. "What I am saying is that here is something whose meaning stands beyond knowledge, barely sustainable therefore in our paltry human terms, for what can we make of such a thing? It points everywhere and nowhere, a series of gateways receding, who knows, perhaps even to the… never ending."

"But this is absurd!" Melichior cried, "This cannot be! That child could die tomorrow, and what then? Pure chance!"

Gathaspah sighed. "True, but what is this death? Is it not too perhaps a gateway?"

Melichior was clearly taken aback. "A Deliverer from death, then?"

Gathaspah shook his head, beginning to laugh a little. "Truly Melichior, I cannot say. But no. From death, no. From life perhaps, through death. I can only guess for I cannot know. Yet for sure the guess holds no less of certainty than what here, now, we profess as certain for us – I mean, of course, the withering leaf, the falling rose, the endless wilting everywhere."

For almost thirty years, those words have haunted me, echoing through the crannies and recesses of my mind; hardly ever more than a whisper, yet enough to have turned these intervening years into this unquiet questing. Ironically, Melichior's affliction when I first knew him in the desert. Not at first, you understand, for there was a time when I could not see beyond the contradiction – I mean the child (even if I had not quite managed to see him) was there, a human being of flesh and blood, with all the needs and helplessness of every other child who was ever in this world.

Gods, whatever else they are, must not be human.

And then again, there was the sudden, ignominious flight, theirs and ours, when Herod, impatient at no news, took it into his head to send a division of his palace guard – a whole division, mind you! – to butcher all the new-born children they could lay their hands on, or so we later heard from travellers along the road. There was scant warning: a hasty scramble, the last-minute collection of coin and anything at all that could be sold (Gathaspah, I remember, even gave some myrrh) so that they should not want along the road or at their journey's end. And they were sent off into the wilderness towards Gaza; God alone knows if they survived the journey. An inauspicious beginning for a king… unthinkable for a god. And we too once more divided our company into many small groups and moved away quickly south and east into the harsh mountain wilderness of Judea.

It was all a very long time ago.

There are times when I have the feeling my life is being lived for me elsewhere, as though this were all a dream. It is but a moment's sensation, like something glimpsed through a crack in the wall, as you pass. When I stride out in the morning, with my shadow going before me, when I trudge back in the evening, and see it diminished, trailing beside me, I wonder about the life of my shadow. But however much you think you seek, these intuitions, these truths – if such indeed they be – it is they that always find you, if at all, not you them.

It was one morning, last winter, when in the cold first light even the sand seemed grey. I had made a fire of thorns and dried camel dung, in the lee of some low, overhanging rocks, a shallow cave, to heat the goat's milk that would take the chill out of my bones. And as I sat in close under the rocks, fixed in my drowsiness by the hypnotic dance of the gathering knot of flame, I became gradually aware of a continual hissing whose insistence gradually drew me out of my comfortable torpor.

At first I thought my pot was cracked and leaking milk into the fire; but it was not so. I moved round to the outer edge of the fire, beneath the lip of the cleft, and as I moved I felt a drop of water cold on my cheek. On the under side of that overhanging rock, small icicles had formed in the night and the growing heat had begun to melt them. The water dripped onto the hot stones enclosing my fire, bubbled in an instant into vapour, and curled up and away and was gone, all in an instant. And where was the ice? Where the water? It hardly mattered. Suddenly, a gate had swung open and there was a pathway leading, who can say where? What was long thought of as panelled and patched, I now know to be seamless.

I have come back here alone after thirty years. And in the town of Qumran, by this dead salt sea, I hear tell of a man living in the wilderness; some say a mad man, others a prophet sent from god – it is ever the way! – and he goes about from place to place proclaiming that the kingdom of heaven is at hand, and baptising with water in his god's name.

I own that I am curious about this man. That he should be hereabouts, with such a message, interests me not a little, for I have long ago come to appreciate the value in coincidence, the triviality of sequence.

I admit, I even find myself wondering if this man was ever in Gaza.